Infallible Two

Starlit Love

Tanishq Maini

To my family, You are the unwavering pillars of my life, the constant source of inspiration.
This book is dedicated to each and every one of you, who has believed in me from the very beginning and encouraged me to chase my dreams.
To my sibling, thank you for being my confidant. Your presence in my life brings joy, laughter, and a sense of camaraderie that fuels my creativity.
To my mentors and teachers, thank you for guiding me, challenging me, and pushing me to explore the depths of my abilities. Your wisdom, expertise, and unwavering dedication to my growth have been invaluable.
To the readers and supporters of my novels and poetry, thank you for joining me on this enchanting ride. Your engagement, feedback, and appreciation for my work fuel my passion and inspire me to continue on this creative path.
This book is a tribute to the love, encouragement, and unwavering support I have received from each and every one of you. It is a celebration of our shared journey, our shared dreams, and our shared love for the written word.

Contents

Prologue

In the sphere where imagination intertwines with reality, where dreams take flight and words shape destinies, lies the beginning of our story. A story that unfolds in the vivid drapes of a young visionary's mind, whose journey bridges the realms of entrepreneurship and novels.

Meet Me, Tanishq Maini, a name that reverberates with ambition and creativity. From the tender age of a teenager, I have emerged as a force to be reckoned with, founding companies that defied conventions and sparked innovation.

But behind the scenes of my bustling ventures, lies another side of me, one that dances in the spheres of rhyme and rhythm. With a pen in hand and the beat of my heart, I breathe life into the lines that captivate audiences. Within these pages, you will witness my meteoric rise, feel the passion that fuels my endeavours, and witness the artistry. Prepare to embark on a journey through the corridors of ambition and creativity, where the ordinary is redefined and the extraordinary is born. Step into my world, where words transcend boundaries, and the power of dreams becomes a tangible reality.

Welcome to the remarkable world of a young visionary who dares to defy expectations and weave my legacy through the pages of time.

Chapter One

Trevor Cartier, drove out onto the quiet street, his mind still buzzing from the vibrant party he had just left behind. The cool midnight air enveloped him, offering a welcome respite from the pulsating music and crowded atmosphere. As he took a moment to collect himself, his gaze wandered aimlessly, until it fell upon a figure standing in the middle of the road.

A woman.

Her presence seemed otherworldly, bathed in the soft glow of the moonlight. Intrigued, Trevor approached her cautiously, his footsteps echoing against the stillness of the night. "H-Hello?" he called out tentatively, unsure if she was lost or in need of assistance. The woman turned, her eyes locking with his. Trevor found himself captivated by their intensity, a mesmerizing shade of emerald green that seemed to hold a universe of secrets. Her dishevelled chestnut hair cascaded down her shoulders, and a faint smile played upon her lips. "I'm sorry," she spoke, her voice a gentle melody that stirred something deep within Trevor. "I didn't mean to startle you. I was just lost in thought." Trevor blinked, his earlier weariness dissipating, replaced by a growing curiosity. "No need to apologise. Are you okay?"

She nodded, her eyes briefly darting away before returning to meet his gaze. "Yes, I am. I was just... taking a moment to clear my head."

He couldn't help but notice the faintest trace of sadness in her voice. "Do you want to talk about it?" Trevor asked, his natural empathy guiding his words. The woman hesitated for a moment, seemingly contemplating his offer. Finally, she nodded. "Perhaps it would be good to share." They moved to the side of the road, finding solace on a nearby park bench.

As they sat down, he introduced himself, extending a hand toward her. "I'm Trevor Cartier." Her expression softened, and she took his hand in a delicate grip. "Delacey Dunne."

Trevor felt a jolt of energy at their touch, as if their connection transcended the realm of ordinary encounters. "It's a pleasure to meet you, Delacey." She smiled, and it was as if the entire world brightened around them.

"Likewise, Trevor."

In that moment, they embarked on a journey, two souls drawn together by the threads of fate. They shared stories of their lives, dreams, and desires. Delacey spoke of her passion for art and her longing to create something that would touch people's hearts. Trevor recounted his adventures and aspirations, his love for music that resonates deep within his soul.

As the night wore on, time lost its meaning, and they found solace in each other's presence. Their conversations flowed effortlessly, unearthing layers of vulnerability, trust, and undeniable chemistry. Trevor realized he had never met someone who understood him so deeply, who made him feel alive in ways he had never experienced before. In the quiet intimacy of that midnight encounter, Trevor and Delacey discovered that the universe had conspired to bring them together. Their meeting was no mere coincidence, it was a prelude to a love story written in the stars. Little did they know that this was only the beginning, the first chapter of a love that would defy all odds and stand as infallible proof that destiny, in its most enchanting form, was real.

Chapter Two

Days turned into weeks, and Trevor and Delacey's connection deepened with each passing moment. They found themselves inseparable, their lives intertwined in a dance of shared experiences and stolen glances. Every stolen moment, every stolen touch, fueled the fire of their affection. In the world of starlit dreams and silver screens, where hearts fluttered with every scene, Trevor found himself drawn to the dazzling allure of Fall Two Productions. A bastion of creativity and passion, it was the empire helmed by none other than the captivating Mr. Gordon, whose eyes held the secrets of a thousand stories. Fate played its hand when the momentous call came in, and it was not Trevor who answered the phone, but the man himself, the enigmatic CEO. The connection was instant, their souls entwining through the invisible wires of destiny. A spark, a whisper of destiny, a silent acknowledgment of something greater at play. Trevor, the dreamer, had poured his heart into the application, weaving his passion for film into the fibers of his resume. As the days turned into an eternal wait, he held his breath, daring to hope that his dreams might take flight.

When the sun finally rose on that fateful morning, Mr. Gordon, now the architect of fate, held the news of Trevor's appointment as the Vice President of Fall Two. A symphony of emotions surged within him, a crescendo of joy and disbelief. To be chosen to stand at the helm of creativity, to steer the course of dreams and inspire others to reach for the stars, it was a rhapsody of the heart. With trembling steps and a heart pounding, he sought out the luminous Delacey, the sun to his moon, to share this once in a lifetime moment.

Beneath the gentle glow of moonlit skies, Trevor found her, radiating her own ethereal beauty, like a goddess among the stars. In that precious moment, he couldn't contain the whirlwind of emotions swirling within. Swept away by the gravity of his joy, he enveloped her in a tender embrace, feeling the warmth of her heart beating in sync with his.

Breathless and elated, he painted the canvas of her mind with the hues of his dreams, describing the cherished offer he had been gifted. "Delacey," he whispered, his voice a symphony of love, "I couldn't have reached this chapter without you. You are my muse, my guiding star, and with you by my side, there are no heights I cannot soar."

Their souls danced like stars in the night sky, hearts bound together by the magic of their shared journey. In each other's eyes, they saw a future brimming with possibilities, where love and ambition intertwined, where they would traverse the filmic tapestry of life hand in hand. Little did they know that their journey had just begun. As they stood there, wrapped in each other's arms, the road ahead promised adventures, challenges, and triumphs that would test the strength of their love. But, armed with the passion that fueled their dreams, they were ready to face whatever life had in store, knowing that their love would be the guiding light leading them through every frame of their mesmerizing tale.

Trevor was overwhelmed with elation, And so, he embarked on his journey towards the workplace nestled amidst the vibrant city of Seattle. As he stepped foot inside the colossal structure that would soon become his domain, he couldn't help but feel a surge of disbelief. The realization that he had been offered the coveted position he had so diligently pursued washed over him like a gentle wave. He made his way to the elevator, accompanied by fellow Fall Two employees, his heart pulsating with anticipation.

Pushing the button for the thirteenth floor, he caught the attention of a fellow passenger. "Hello," a voice chimed in, belonging to Ariana. Trevor reciprocated the greeting, a smile dancing on his lips. Curiosity getting the better of her, Ariana inquired, "Are you a recent addition to our ranks?" Trevor nodded affirmatively, his eyes gleaming with pride.

Just then, the elevator doors slid open, revealing the grandeur of Mr. Gordon's office, a sight that left him awestruck. "Welcome, Mr. Trevor!" boomed Mr. Gordon's commanding voice, resonating through the room. Trevor could hardly believe his ears. It seemed that Mr. Gordon had personally reached out to him, making the call that would alter the course of his life. As he stepped further into Mr. Gordon's office, he couldn't help but marvel at its opulence. The walls adorned with exquisite artwork, the bookshelves filled with leather-bound tomes, and the large mahogany desk commanding the center of the room all exuded an aura of success and power.

Trevor took a deep breath, trying to compose himself as he walked towards the imposing figure behind the desk. "Thank you, Mr. Gordon," he replied, trying to steady his voice. "It's an honour to be here, and I'm truly grateful for this opportunity." Mr. Gordon, a man in his late fifties with a strong, authoritative presence, smiled warmly. "The honour is all mine, Trevor. We've been following your career closely, and your dedication and skills have not gone unnoticed."

As they exchanged pleasantries, Trevor couldn't help but feel a mix of excitement and nervousness. This position was a dream come true, but he knew that it came with great responsibility and high expectations.

Mr. Gordon gestured for Trevor to take a seat across from him. "Now, let's talk about your role here," Mr. Gordon said, leaning back in his chair. "As the new Head of Innovation, you'll be responsible for spearheading new projects, exploring groundbreaking ideas, and driving Fall Two to even greater heights. Your previous achievements demonstrate that you're more than capable of taking on this challenge."

Trevor nodded, absorbing every word. He had envisioned a position where he could make a real impact, and it seemed that this was it.

"We take pride in fostering a culture of innovation and growth here at Fall Two," Mr. Gordon continued. "And I believe you're the perfect fit for our organization. I've seen your passion for pushing boundaries and your ability to inspire others around you."

"Thank you, Mr. Gordon," Trevor said humbly. "I'll do my best to live up to the trust you've placed in me."

"I have no doubt about that," Mr. Gordon replied with a reassuring nod. "I've called you here today not only to offer you this position but also to extend my personal support. Feel free to reach out to me whenever you need guidance or assistance."

The weight of Mr. Gordon's words settled in Trevor's mind. This was a rare opportunity, and he knew he needed to seize it. From that moment on, he was determined to leave a lasting impact on the company and the world.

› Chapter Three

As Trevor delved into his new role at Fall Two, he found
a sense of belonging among his colleagues. Ariana, the
fellow employee he had met in the elevator, became a close
ally. Her experience and insights helped him navigate the
company's inner workings, and their friendship grew as
they collaborated on numerous projects.
Under Trevor's leadership, the company flourished.
Innovative products and services flowed from his team,
capturing the attention of the market and propelling Fall
Two to the forefront of their industry. His dedication,
along with the unwavering support of Mr. Gordon and the
team, made the company's future look brighter than ever.
But success didn't come without challenges. Trevor faced
moments of doubt, questioning if he was up to the task.
However, each time he found himself on the verge of giving
in to uncertainty, he remembered Mr. Gordon's words of
encouragement and the unwavering belief that he could
achieve greatness.
As the day drew to a close, Trevor couldn't wait to return
home, his heart brimming with eagerness and affection.
With a loving anticipation, he approached Delacey's door,
knowing that behind it, his world would come alive with
her presence. As the door opened, there she stood, a vision
of grace and warmth, her smile illuminating his weary
soul. Without hesitation, Trevor pulled her close, planting

a tender kiss on her forehead, and enveloped her in a tight embrace. "I missed you," he whispered softly, his voice a gentle caress against her ear.

Delacey's heart swelled with happiness, feeling his love engulfing her like a cozy blanket. In the haven of their shared home, Delacey had prepared a special dinner, a labour of love dedicated to the man who held her heart. They sat together, side by side, savouring the meal and the moments, as Trevor animatedly shared the tales of his day. Delacey listened intently, captivated by his every word, knowing that her presence had made a difference in his world.

As the night wore on, the atmosphere was charged with an intimate connection that words could barely describe. When Trevor turned his gaze to her, the way his eyes held a mixture of admiration and love sent her heart aflutter. Delacey's fingers danced across his skin, as if creating a symphony of emotions that only they could hear. With a loving gesture, Trevor rested his head upon Delacey's lap, finding comfort and solace in her tender touch. They reveled in the ordinary, intertwining their lives with a beautiful simplicity that made each moment more magical than the last.

The next morning arrived, and the soft melody of an alarm awakened Delacey. As she scrolled through her phone, a message from her past surfaced, but she brushed it aside, choosing to cherish the love and happiness she had found with Trevor. With a warm embrace and gentle kisses on his cheeks, she expressed her love, a silent promise that the past could never intrude upon their blissful present.

Their passion ignited like an eternal flame, and they shared a romantic interlude that left their hearts entwined in ecstasy. Afterwards, they bathed together, their connection deepening in the intimate closeness they shared. As they danced to the rhythm of their hearts, they prepared breakfast with laughter and joy, a seamless symphony of love.

Trevor couldn't help but admire Delacey's caring nature and boundless charm. In a moment of enchantment, she playfully snapped her fingers, but he was already lost in thoughts of her, completely captivated by her presence.

As the sun kissed the horizon, Trevor embarked on his daily journey to work, cruising through the bustling downtown streets, the rhythm of hip-hop music filling his car with energy and anticipation.

Just as he was getting into the groove, a call from Mr. Gordon interrupted his musical reverie, urging him to attend an urgent meeting in his absence due to an unplanned vacation. Caught in the labyrinth of traffic, Trevor felt a tinge of anxiety in his voice, the weight of responsibility pressing on his shoulders. Determined to make it to the office on time, he honked his horn with fervour, seeking a path through the congested roads. In a moment of triumph, the traffic parted, and he swiftly parked his car, rushing to the conference room where the meeting awaited.

With composure and grace, he introduced himself as the company's Vice President, seamlessly stepping into the role Mr. Gordon entrusted him with. Impressing the board members with his sharp wit and charisma, Trevor deftly navigated the meeting, addressing the company's challenges with wisdom and insight. As the room buzzed with conversation, he unveiled a brilliant plan that garnered praise and admiration, elevating both the business and his own reputation in the eyes of his colleagues. Basking in the glow of a successful conclusion,

Trevor left the meeting room with a triumphant grin, taking a deep breath of accomplishment. Back in his cabin, he continued to work diligently, determined to make his mark in the world of business and passion.

However, as evening approached, an unexpected hurdle presented itself. When Trevor made his way to the parking lot, he discovered his car with a flat tire, and frustration surged within him. Calling the local car dealer for assistance, he arranged for a tow and repairs, choosing to take a taxi home for the time being.

Arriving at his house, he expected to find solace in Delacey's embrace. Yet, to his surprise, the door was locked, and a sense of unease washed over him. Using the phone key to unlock the door, he stepped inside, only to find Delacey's absence, leaving him bewildered and yearning for her comforting presence. As the night draped its mystery over them, Trevor's heart was filled with questions, wondering where his beloved Delacey could be.

Chapter Four

Delacey didn't respond when Trevor called her repeatedly throughout the night. The following morning, Trevor woke up blanked out. He had his office, but he was unable to focus on anything since he was preoccupied with wondering how and where Delacey would be. As a result, he called out Ariana, one of his coworkers. Since he had a serious case to tackle today, he asked her to manage his work.

"Definitely, I will," Ariana retorted. As she hangs up the phone, she says,

"Please take care of yourself and if you need anything, I'll be right here to assist you."

Trevor immediately leaves for the locations Delacey once told him she cherished the most. He persistently searched for her, but his efforts to locate her were in vain.

He then went back to his residence while still having questions for Delacey. Using his phone, he locates Delacey, and when he pulls over to the site, he discovers that Delacey had been with her ex the entire night. He knocks on the door, and when the door was opened, Delacey and her ex were there. When they are all reunited, Trevor retorts to Delacey, "Couldn't you tell me, is this what I deserved?"

He knocks on the door before leaving, driving off to a bar where he consumes far more alcohol than usual. Trevor accepted an impressionable women's offer to join her in dancing but he starts to feel uneasy and drives back home inebriated. He speeds recklessly down the street, but makes it safely home. Following that, he uses his phone to access the door and resumes his search for alcohol, yet comes up empty-handed once again. Trevor cried and lost consciousness when he realized that he had lost Delacey. He falls asleep on the couch itself.

As dawn breaks, he stirs from slumber and reaches for his phone, only to discover it devoid of any notifications. Trevor believed that Delacey and him had split up, but he continued to hold out hope and drove to his office, and got carried away with his usual routine.

Trevor had been driving back to his home after a long day at work. As he usually did on his way back, he stopped off at the 24/7 convenience store to pick up his usual can of beer and a few snacks. Satisfied with his purchase, he jumped back into his car and started driving off. But something was different this time. He wasn't feeling like going home yet. Perhaps it was the beer, or perhaps he just needed an escape from the few things that happened with him. He drove off onto the highway, pushing the speed limit and letting the wind blow through his hair. Within moments, he was going way faster than he should be. As he turned a sharp curve, he suddenly noticed a big tree standing in the middle of the road. He quickly slammed on the brakes, but it was too late. He crashed right into the tree.

Trevor awoke to find himself in a hospital bed, with a broken leg and minor bruises. It had been a close call, and one he wouldn't easily forget. Trevor groaned as he opened his eyes for the first time since the accident. He tried to move his body, wincing in pain as he felt the tightness of the bandages that surrounded his casted leg. A wave of fear crashed over him that he had been in an accident. He couldn't remember what happened or how he got here.

As he started to panic, a nurse walked in. "Ah, there you are," the nurse said with a warm smile. "You gave us quite the scare, Trevor. But you're going to be okay now, I promise."

Trevor took the nurse's words to heart and started piecing together what happened. He remembered a car accident, his car had gone out of control and he had crashed into a tree. While he was okay for the most part, his leg had clearly taken a beating and was now broken. Trevor was grateful that he was alive, and that his injuries weren't too severe. He vowed to himself to never take a risk like that again. The nurse patted his arm in reassurance before she left the room. He was thankful for the doctors and nurses who had tended to him. He knew he would be okay now, and he was ready to move on and start rebuilding his life.

He now had spent months in the hospital, surrounded by the nurses and doctors who had cared for him during his lengthy recovery. Their kindness and patience had been a lifeline to Trevor during these dark days. He had thanked them from the bottom of his heart for the compassion they had shown in the midst of his suffering. While he had been on the bed for months, Mr. Gordon came to know about him and reached out to him immediately. Mr. Gordon remarked, "How did this happen and you should have at least asked anyone to inform us? We might have borne all your expenses," but it had been too late as Trevor had already paid off all the expenses for the hospital. Now, after months of healing, he was finally ready to go home.

He was relieved that he had made it through, and knew that a new chapter in his life was about to begin. As he stepped through the hospital doors, Trevor drew in a deep breath of fresh air, feeling the warmth of the sun on his skin and the wind blowing through his hair. He was ready to start rebuilding his life. He would throw himself into his work, immersing himself in projects that felt meaningful and rewarding. He would also try to make time in his life for the people he cared about, reconnecting with old friends and nurturing relationships with family. Finally, he would try to make time for himself, focusing on self-care and taking steps to build better physical and mental health. He knew that this time he wouldn't take his health for granted, he was thankful for every moment, and would strive to make the most of the second chance he had been given. He started on with his new life by waking up at 4.00am, starting with workouts on a daily basis every day twice, morning and evening, after which he swam for at least 2 hours and which was then followed by his usual office routine.

Chapter Five

While he was getting ready to leave for his first day after the fatal accident he had faced due to his unconsciousness, the bell rings. Trevor then moves ahead to unlock the door and he sees Delacey, standing right there with tears in her eyes. Trevor could not resist himself and wiped off her tears and asked her to get in, Delacey then apologised for everything that she did, and Trevor listened to her carefully, while having many questions for Delacey. He then asked Delacey to stay here until he returns back from his office, as he was already late and needed to catch up with a lot of things. He kissed Delacey on her forehead and left for his office.

As he entered the office he saw Ariana holding a bunch of flowers, he wondered what was happening in the office, but then suddenly Mr. Gordon came out, personally and offered that very bunch of flowers to him, he was overwhelmed, and everyone welcomed him and prayed for a speedy recovery for him. Moreover, As Mr. Gordon was about to turn 60 and it was nearly the time for him to retire, he then announced that the next appointed CEO was Trevor. Mr. Gordon, the CEO of a mid-sized company, was about to celebrate his 60th birthday. It was a time for him to start thinking about the next phase of his life which, for most people in his position, meant retirement. He had spent nearly forty years in the business sector, and thought it was time for him to step down and allow someone else to take on the mantle of leadership.

At his birthday celebration, Mr. Gordon took the opportunity to thank his colleagues and staff for their years of service and success. He then announced that he was stepping down, and that the new appointed CEO was Trevor. Trevor had been with the company for a few months. Having started out as a Vice President, he worked his way up through the ranks, quickly proving his worth by taking the lead on several successful projects. It became clear that his skills and talents would be valuable to the company for the future. As Mr. Gordon stepped down, he knew that while he was leaving the company, he had left it in capable hands. He believed that Trevor had the vision and ability to lead the company to further success over the coming years and wished him all the best in his new role.

Trevor, now in a position of tremendous responsibility, knew that he had some big shoes to fill. He was anxious and excited to get to work and continue to build on the success of the past. With tremendous support from the board of directors, the staff, and Mr. Gordon himself, Trevor had every confidence he could lead the company into a bright future. All that was left to do was roll up his sleeves and put all his plans into action! Trevor gathered the senior team and together they discussed key areas of the company and the best plan of action to improve them. He was highly respected amongst the team and everyone could see his ambition and enthusiasm for the company. He was ready to not only strengthen their existing product range but most importantly to update and create new products and services for their customers. He also wanted to create an improved online presence for the company and create a platform that could spur even further growth and success.

With his plans in place and his team of experienced leadership ready to begin, Trevor was confident of the bright future ahead, and he was ready to roll up his sleeves and put everything into action. It seemed that a brighter future for the company was just around the corner. Trevor had worked hard to get to the top and today he had been given the chance to make it happen. As the CEO of a booming business, Trevor had taken over Mr. Gordon's seat with a wave of excitement and anticipation. Though his emotions were conflicted, he was eager to take on the responsibility and committed to make things work.

Trevor had put in long hours, he leaned back in his chair, looking out across the cabin with a new found confidence and a sense of accomplishment. He was filled with joy and happiness at the thought that he had made his dreams come true. He left the office with a smile on his face and headed home to relax and enjoy the evening. He was pleasantly surprised to find a stack of mail waiting for him on the table. He eagerly opened them up one by one, each containing good news from potential partners around the globe. This was the start of something, Trevor thought. He had made something of himself, and after a long and tiring day, it was good to head home, with the knowledge that he was working hard for something great. As he sleeplessly trudged down the streets, the sunset illuminated the streets with an orange haze, Trevor allowed himself to pause and feel satisfied with the hard work he had done. He was in the middle of something grand, something that he would leave a lasting impact on the world. He continued to head home, sure in the knowledge that he had begun the journey of a lifetime. He was going to take what he had started and make it bigger, better, and more beautiful. He was proud, exhausted, and determined to keep going. This was only the beginning, Trevor thought, and he couldn't wait to see where his future would take him.

As he returned home and unlocked the door with his phone and saw Delacey sleeping on the couch. He hesitated before waking her, carefully crouching down by her side and pressing a kiss to her forehead. Delacey stirred, eyes fluttering open. He smiled before wrapping his arms around her, lifting her from the couch and carrying her to the bedroom. Gently he tucked her under the warm blankets, watching her as she drifted off to sleep. When he finally turned to leave, Delacey's hand reached out and grabbed his. He stopped to turn back, holding her hand in his and offering her a comforting kiss. He traced soothing circles over her fingers, lightly punctuating each movement with a sweet kiss. With a final pat on Delacey's forehead, Trevor smiled and stepped away from the bed, happy that he could provide Delacey with the safety and security she deserved. His heart was filled with hope as he thought of their future, filled with exciting possibilities.

Chapter Six

In the morning light, Delacey awoke in her familiar bed, feeling an unusual sense of rejuvenation and contentment. Surprisingly, she found Trevor on her couch, having somehow made his way there during the night and drifted into slumber. Gazing at the picturesque scene, she pressed a gentle kiss to his forehead and nestled closely beside him, seeking solace in his embrace. There was an unexplainable energy simmering between them, an enigmatic connection that defied words.

As the day unfolded, she prepared a delectable breakfast and shared with him the reasons behind her presence on the road when they had crossed paths. She recounted the tragic incident involving her boyfriend, how his inexplicable anger had erupted into baseless accusations and hurtful yelling. Her helplessness in the face of his outburst had left her humiliated and wounded. What cut even deeper were his parting nonsensical remarks. Despite all this pain, she had returned to him, driven by a force she couldn't quite understand.

Trevor's eyes conveyed understanding, and he enveloped her in a comforting embrace. His whispered words carried solace and empowerment, urging her never to tolerate such treatment and reminding her that the choice to return to him was hers alone.

His words resonated within her, infusing her with

newfound strength and courage. The realisation dawned upon her that she was an individual with agency, capable of making her own decisions. Surprisingly, life seemed to regain its equilibrium. Her heart felt lighter, as though a burden had been lifted, she had finally stood up for herself, asserting her identity and worth. Love for Trevor bloomed anew, stronger than before. With a nod and a faint smile playing on her lips, they embarked on their shared journey. Delacey had, at last, taken the decisive step she had long yearned for.

Together, Delacey and Trevor navigated the path ahead with a shared sense of purpose and newfound determination. Their connection deepened, fueled by mutual respect and the strength they drew from each other. The struggles of the past seemed to fade into insignificance as they embraced a future defined by their own choices.

As days turned into weeks, Delacey's confidence continued to grow. She pursued her passions with unwavering dedication, channelling her energy into her pursuits and ventures. Trevor stood by her side as a pillar of unwavering support, offering encouragement and advice whenever needed. With his guidance, she honed her entrepreneurial skills and innovative ideas, giving life to her visions in ways she had never imagined.

Their relationship flourished in an environment of open communication and shared dreams. They cherished the moments of laughter and vulnerability, creating a space where each could be truly themselves without fear of judgement. Delacey discovered a sense of liberation she hadn't thought possible, freed from the constraints of her past and the suffocating expectations that had once held her captive. One evening, as the sun dipped below the horizon, casting a warm glow over the world around them, Trevor took Delacey's hand and led her to a spot where they could watch the colours of the sky blend in harmony. With a gentle smile, he spoke of their journey, reflecting on how far they had come as individuals and as a couple.

"We've overcome challenges that seemed insurmountable," he said, his voice a soothing melody. "And in doing so, we've crafted a story that's uniquely ours."

Delacey's eyes sparkled as she leaned against him, feeling the rhythm of his heart echoing her own sentiments. "It's a story of growth, of finding strength within ourselves and in each other," she added, her voice resonating with gratitude.

He pulled her closer, wrapping his arms around her in a protective embrace. "And it's a story that's still being written," he whispered. "With every step we take, we're shaping our own narrative, one of empowerment, love, and shared dreams."

As they stood there, bathed in the fading light, Delacey knew that her journey had taken an unexpected and beautiful turn. With Trevor by her side, she had discovered the power of self-belief and the joy of embracing innovation and ingenuity in all aspects of life.

Chapter Seven

Trevor meticulously organises a corporate occasion to commemorate the 5th anniversary of his enterprise, Fall Two Inc. As the preparations for the event unfold, Trevor finds himself immersed in a whirlwind of tasks and decisions. With his keen eye for detail and his commitment to perfection, he leaves no stone unturned in ensuring that every aspect of the occasion is flawlessly executed.

Invitations are sent out to industry leaders, partners, and clients who have been instrumental in the success of Fall Two Inc. over the past five years. The venue is carefully chosen, a stunning blend of modern architecture and elegant decor that reflects the company's innovative spirit. Trevor personally oversees the menu, selecting a fusion of delectable cuisines that mirrors the diverse and dynamic nature of his business ventures.

As the day of the event approaches, Trevor's anticipation grows. He knows that this celebration is not only about marking a milestone, it's a testament to the dedication and hard work he and his team have poured into building Fall Two Inc. from the ground up. The company's journey has been marked by challenges, breakthroughs, and countless late nights, and this event symbolizes the culmination of those efforts.

On the day of the anniversary celebration, the atmosphere is electric. Guests arrive dressed in their finest attire, a blend of sophistication and style that mirrors the ethos of Trevor's ventures.

The event kicks off with a heartfelt speech from Trevor, in which he reflects on the journey, expresses gratitude to everyone who contributed, and shares his vision for the future. Throughout the evening, guests engage in lively conversations, forging new connections and strengthening existing relationships. Trevor moves through the crowd, effortlessly weaving between discussions about technology, fashion, and entrepreneurship, the three pillars that define his ventures. The night is filled with laughter, inspiration, and a shared sense of achievement.

As the event draws to a close, Trevor stands amidst the crowd, a sense of contentment washing over him. The celebration has not only honoured the past but has also set the stage for the next chapter of innovation and growth. With a renewed sense of purpose, Trevor looks ahead, knowing that the journey is far from over. And as he gazes at the city skyline beyond, he envisions the future his ventures will shape, one that embraces innovation and ingenuity in all its forms. And presents the inclusion of a new enterprise.

Amidst the fading echoes of applause and the soft hum of satisfied conversation, Trevor takes a moment to savour the achievement. The celebration has been a resounding success, a symphony of elegance and ambition that he had meticulously orchestrated.

But as the final notes of the event linger in the air, he's reminded that the rhythm of progress is relentless, and the next verse of his journey is waiting to be written.

As the night winds down, Trevor exchanges warm farewells with his guests, feeling a deep connection with each person who has been a part of this evening.

Industry titans, creative minds, and visionaries have converged under his roof, and he's determined to nurture these connections into partnerships that will shape the landscape of business and innovation.

Once the venue starts to empty, Trevor retreats to a quiet corner, allowing himself a moment of solitude. He gazes out through the floor-to-ceiling windows, his thoughts dancing between the past, present, and future. The city skyline glows in the distance, a tapestry of dreams and possibilities that he's determined to weave into his ventures.

A familiar voice interrupts his reverie. It's Ava, his longtime friend, who has been by his side through every twist and turn of his entrepreneurial journey. Her smile is both reassuring and inquisitive, and he knows she's the perfect person to share his latest idea with.

"Trevor," she begins, her voice a mixture of curiosity and encouragement, "you've achieved something remarkable tonight. Fall Two Inc. has reached heights that many only dream of. What's on your mind now?"

Trevor turns to Ava, a spark of excitement in his eyes. "Ava, you know how much this celebration means to me. But as we stand here, surrounded by the fruits of our labour, I can't help but envision the next chapter."

Ava nods, intrigued. "Tell me more."

Trevor's gaze returns to the skyline, his expression a mix of determination and possibility. "I've realized that our ventures, as successful as they are, have touched only certain aspects of people's lives. Technology, fashion, and entrepreneurship are significant, but there's more out there, unexplored territories where innovation can make a difference."

Ava leans in, her curiosity deepening. "Are you thinking of

a new venture?"

Trevor smiles, the fire of his vision burning brighter. "Yes. Imagine a space where technology and fashion converge in ways that haven't been seen before. An enterprise that isn't just about products, but experiences. An inclusive platform that empowers individuals to express themselves, to embrace their uniqueness through technology-infused fashion."

Ava's eyes widen with understanding. "You're talking about breaking boundaries, about reinventing the very concept of self-expression."

Trevor nods, his excitement contagious. "Exactly. I want to create a world where wearable technology isn't just functional, it's a form of art. Where fashion isn't confined to fabric, it's a canvas for innovation. And most importantly, where every individual feels seen and celebrated for who they are."

Ava's expression softens with admiration. "Trevor, you've always had a way of seeing the future before it arrives. This idea, it's audacious, but that's what makes it beautiful. It's a chance to touch lives in ways we haven't even imagined."

As the night gives way to the first rays of dawn, Trevor's heart beats in sync with the rhythm of possibility. The 5th-anniversary celebration was a moment of reflection, of honouring the journey that brought him here. But now, as he embarks on the dawn of a new venture, one that promises to transcend boundaries and embrace the ever-changing nature of innovation, he knows that his journey is far from over. The skyline that stretches before him is no longer just a view, it's a canvas on which he'll paint his dreams, one daring stroke at a time. With Ava by his side and the echoes of celebration still ringing in his ears, Trevor steps forward into the embrace of the future, ready to make his mark once again.

Months pass since that momentous anniversary celebration, and Trevor's vision takes tangible form as he pours his energy into his new venture. The headquarters of InFall, as he names it, buzzes with creativity and collaboration. Teams of designers, engineers, and artists huddle around sleek workstations, bringing to life the fusion of fashion and technology that Trevor envisions.

The journey isn't without challenges. Developing cutting-edge wearable technology that seamlessly integrates into fashion requires constant experimentation and refinement. But Trevor's unwavering commitment to perfection, his ability to inspire those around him, and his knack for attracting the brightest minds in various fields ensure that progress continues, one breakthrough at a time.

Ava, as his partner, stands by his side throughout the process. Her analytical mind complements his visionary thinking, and together, they make decisions that shape the company's direction. Their synergy sets a tone of collaboration and inclusivity, echoing the very values that InFall seeks to promote.

As prototypes turn into functional products, Trevor takes a step that resonates with the spirit of his ventures, he decides to unveil the new line at an experiential event like no other. The stage is set for the "Infall Unveil Gala," an occasion that fuses fashion, technology, and art into a spectacle that captures the essence of InFall.

Invitations are extended to a diverse array of individuals, not just industry elites, but also artists, activists, and thinkers who embody the ethos of innovation and self-expression. The venue is a symphony of light and sound, a testament to the seamless integration of creativity and technology. Attendees marvel at the futuristic fashion pieces on display, garments that pulse with light, change colour at a touch, and respond to the wearer's emotions.

When Trevor takes the stage for his opening speech, the room falls into a hushed silence. "Welcome to the InFall Unveil Gala," he begins, his voice carrying a blend of gratitude and determination. "Tonight, we come together to witness a new chapter in the world of fashion and technology, a chapter that isn't just about innovation, but about celebrating who we are."

His words resonate deeply with the audience, and as the event unfolds, guests engage in immersive experiences that blur the lines between art and technology. Fashion-shows become showcases of individuality, where models of all backgrounds strut down the runway, each wearing a piece that uniquely reflects their personality.

As the night reaches its peak, Trevor finds himself immersed in conversations that extend far beyond business. Attendees share their stories of empowerment, how the fusion of fashion and technology has allowed them to express themselves in ways they never thought possible. Ideas flow, connections form, and a sense of shared purpose fills the air.

As the InFall Unveil Gala draws to a close, Trevor stands once again in the midst of a contented crowd. The applause that surrounds him isn't just for the success of the event or the innovative products unveiled, it's a recognition of the impact that his ventures have on people's lives.

As he looks out at the city skyline beyond, a smile tugs at the corners of Trevor's lips. The journey that started with Fall Two Inc. has now blossomed into something even more profound, a movement that redefines self-expression, challenges conventions, and embraces the boundless potential of innovation. And as he gazes ahead at the horizon of possibilities, he knows that his ventures are not just about creating products, but about shaping a future where every individual can boldly wear their uniqueness and inspire others to do the same.

Chapter Eight

In the days following the InFall Unveil Gala, Trevor and Ava find themselves reflecting on the remarkable journey they've embarked upon. Their venture, InFall, has garnered attention not only for its groundbreaking products but also for the philosophy it represents, a philosophy of celebrating diversity, embracing technology, and fostering a sense of empowerment.

The media buzz surrounding the gala reverberates throughout the industry and beyond. Magazine covers, television features, and online articles all highlight the fusion of fashion and technology that InFall has pioneered. And yet, amidst the accolades, Trevor remains grounded, understanding that the true measure of success isn't just about headlines, it's about the impact his creations have on the lives of individuals.

One morning, as Trevor and Ava sit in his office, overlooking the city that has witnessed their journey, Ava poses a question that has been lingering in her mind. "Trevor, you've achieved so much already. What's the driving force behind your constant pursuit of innovation?" Trevor leans back in his chair, a thoughtful expression on his face. "Ava, when I started this journey, it was about creating something unique, something that could change the way people perceive and interact with the world. But over time, it's become more than that. It's become a responsibility, a responsibility to use innovation to uplift, to empower, and to bridge gaps."

Ava nods, understanding the weight of his words. "It's about using your influence to make a difference."

Trevor smiles, the passion in his eyes unwavering. "Exactly. Our ventures have always been about more than just profit. They've been about leaving a mark, about inspiring others to dream bigger, to challenge norms, and to embrace the power of self-expression. InFall is a manifestation of that philosophy, a platform that not only offers cutting-edge products but also nurtures a community of individuals who are valiant to express themselves."

Ava's gaze is filled with admiration, "You've certainly succeeded in creating that community. And I have no doubt that your impact will continue to grow."

In the weeks that follow, InFall continues to expand its reach, with collaborations that blur the lines between technology, art, and fashion. The venture partners with artists to create interactive installations that showcase the possibilities of wearable tech, hosts workshops that teach individuals how to integrate technology into their creative projects, and collaborates with organizations that work towards fostering inclusivity and diversity.

Trevor's dedication to his vision attracts attention from unexpected quarters. A renowned university reaches out, expressing interest in partnering with InFall to establish a program that combines design, technology, and entrepreneurship. The idea of nurturing the next generation of innovators resonates deeply with Trevor, and he eagerly takes on this new challenge.

As he addresses the students during the inaugural class of the program, Trevor's words reflect the journey he's undertaken and the principles that guide him. "Innovation is not just about creating something new," he tells them. "It's about creating something that has the power to inspire, to change perspectives, and to create a positive impact. Embrace the uncharted territory, challenge the boundaries, and never forget the potential you hold to shape the future."

With every passing day, Trevor's ventures evolve, his influence rippling outwards to touch lives and shape the landscape of innovation. As he looks ahead at the horizon of endless possibilities, he knows that this journey is far from over. The city skyline continues to be his canvas, and he's determined to paint it with strokes of empowerment, diversity, and innovation that will leave an indelible mark on generations to come.

In the midst of his ongoing ventures, Trevor remains true to his principles, leading InFall with an unwavering commitment to his vision. He nurtures a culture of collaboration within the company, fostering an environment where individuals from diverse backgrounds and fields of expertise come together to push the boundaries of what's possible. The company's workspace becomes a hub of creativity, where ideas flow freely, and innovation thrives.

One day, as Trevor walks through the bustling office, he overhears a group of designers discussing a new project. They're brainstorming ways to integrate sustainable materials into their wearable technology, a direction that aligns perfectly with InFall' commitment to positive social and environmental impact. Trevor joins the conversation, his passion for innovation evident in his every word.

"Imagine," he says, leaning in, "if we could not only redefine how people interact with technology but also contribute to a more sustainable future. Let's weave together aesthetics, functionality, and ethics into our designs."

The designers' eyes light up as they absorb his words, and the conversation takes a new, inspired direction. This idea becomes the catalyst for a groundbreaking initiative within the company, an initiative that seeks to revolutionize the way technology and fashion intersect with sustainability.

As months pass, InFall unveils a line of products that utilise recycled and eco-friendly materials, demonstrating that fashion-forward technology can coexist harmoniously with environmental consciousness. The response is overwhelmingly positive, with consumers and industry peers alike applauding the company's commitment to responsible innovation.

Trevor's dedication to his vision also extends beyond the walls of his company. He becomes an advocate for the integration of technology education in schools, partnering with educational organizations to provide resources and mentorship to aspiring young minds. His efforts aim to empower the next generation with the tools they need to shape a future that's driven by both creativity and innovation.

The success of InFall opens new doors for Trevor's ventures. He's invited to speak at international conferences, where he shares his insights on the future of technology and fashion. His talks are a blend of inspiring narratives and practical advice, encouraging others to embrace the unknown, challenge conventions, and create a positive impact through their work.

Through it all, Ava remains his constant source of support and insight. Their partnership stands as a testament to the power of collaboration and the strength that comes from sharing a vision. They weather challenges together, celebrate triumphs together, and their bond serves as a foundation upon which their ventures thrive.

As years go by, Trevor continues to look ahead, always seeking new frontiers to explore, new horizons to shape. The city skyline that once symbolized his dreams has become a backdrop to a legacy that he's building, one that encompasses innovation, empowerment, and a celebration of individuality. And as he gazes out at that ever-changing skyline, he knows that his journey, marked by its challenges, triumphs, and boundless creativity, is a story that will continue to inspire and ignite the sparks of innovation in others.

As Trevor's ventures evolve and his impact deepens, he finds himself at a crossroads once again, faced with a decision that could shape the next phase of his journey. InFall has become a beacon of responsible innovation, but Trevor knows that true progress requires not just individual success, but systemic change. With this realization, a new idea begins to take root in his mind, a vision that extends beyond his ventures and into the heart of a broader movement.

He gathers his team, Ava by his side, to discuss this new direction. "We've accomplished so much together," he begins, his voice a blend of determination and hope. "But I believe it's time to inspire change on a larger scale. Our ventures have shown what's possible, and now, let's channel our energy into fostering a community of innovators, a collective that's dedicated to reshaping industries and driving positive transformation."

Ava nods, her eyes reflecting the fire of Trevor's vision. "You're talking about creating a platform for collaboration, for those who share our values and want to make a lasting impact."

Trevor smiles, his gaze focused on a future he's ready to seize. "Exactly. I want to establish the Innovator's Nexus, a space where minds converge, where ideas spark, and where innovation takes root. A platform that supports not just our ventures, but a network of enterprises that are committed to innovation, sustainability, and social responsibility."

The team members exchange excited glances, and the room fills with a sense of shared purpose. The vision of the Innovator's Nexus begins to take shape, a hub where entrepreneurs, thinkers, and visionaries come together to exchange ideas, collaborate on projects, and drive change that transcends industries.

Months later, the Innovator's Nexus becomes a reality. A physical space with a global reach, it hosts events, workshops, and summits that bring together individuals who are driven by a common goal: to make a positive impact through innovation. The Nexus becomes a melting pot of creativity and collaboration, where entrepreneurs from diverse backgrounds connect, share insights, and forge partnerships that span continents.

Trevor and Ava stand at the heart of this dynamic space, surrounded by the hum of passionate conversations and the energy of possibility. As they address a gathering of innovators, Trevor's voice carries the resonance of his journey and the lessons he's learned.

"We stand here not just as entrepreneurs, but as stewards of a movement," he tells the audience. "The Innovator's Nexus is a testament to the fact that innovation knows no boundaries, that it's a force that can shape industries, challenge norms, and create a better world. As we collaborate, as we dream big, let's remember that our impact isn't just about us, it's about the ripple effect that our actions create."

With each passing day, the Innovator's Nexus grows stronger, fostering a community that is bound by a shared commitment to driving positive change. Entrepreneurs, activists, and thought leaders converge to share their stories, their expertise, and their collective passion for innovation that transforms lives.

Trevor's journey, marked by its milestones and the dreams that were woven into reality, continues to inspire generations. The city skyline that once served as a backdrop to his aspirations now bears witness to a legacy that reaches far beyond individual success, a legacy that has shaped industries, empowered individuals, and ignited a movement of innovation that will forever transform the landscape of possibility. And as he looks ahead, he knows that the story of innovation, collaboration, and progress is one that will continue to be written, one innovation at a time.

Chapter Nine

One fine day, Trevor found himself near Ava's cabin when he caught snippets of Ava's conversation with Ariana. They were discussing the dramatic downfall of Fall Two Inc. Later, about an hour passed, and Trevor was engrossed in his phone when a buzz from Ariana, the CEO of Fall Two Inc, captured his attention. She reached out to Trevor for assistance. Responding affirmatively, Trevor inquired about the nature of her request. Ariana explained that Fall Two had crumbled since his departure and expressed a desperate need to rectify the situation.

Trevor promptly agreed to help and set about arranging a meeting between Ariana and the Fall Two Inc. team, enlisting Ava's aid in the process. As the day waned, Trevor left the scene in his opulent sports car, heading home. To his surprise, Delacey had prepared a charming candlelit dinner at home, a heartfelt gesture after his long day of work. In the cozy ambiance, they swayed to the music, Trevor's hand securely caressing a testament to the unspoken bond they shared.

As the night deepened, their laughter and playful banter evolved into a dance of raw passion. A soft symphony of sighs and gasps painted the air, accompanied by the gentle rustling of sheets as they explored the depths of their connection. Their souls intertwined, weaving a story of vulnerability and trust, of two individuals unafraid to expose their true selves to each other.

The candlelight continued to flicker, casting playful shadows that danced upon the walls, mirroring the ebb and flow of their ardour. The world outside may have been unaware of this cocoon of intimacy they had created, a sanctuary where vulnerability blossomed into unbridled ecstasy.

And as the first rays of dawn brushed the sky, painting it with hues of pink and gold, they lay tangled in each other's arms, breathing in sync, their bodies a canvas of shared moments. The night had been a chapter written in the ink of passion, a testament to the timeless tale of love found in stolen moments and whispered promises. With the gradual brightening of the room, reality tiptoed back into their haven of intimacy. They exchanged sleepy smiles, their eyes were carrying the glimmer of the night's enchantment. The world beckoned beyond the windows, but for now, they lingered in the cocoon they had woven.

As the morning sun painted warmth upon their entangled forms, they spoke not only through words but through the silent understanding that bound them. It was a language of shared vulnerability, a code only they comprehended, a bridge connecting their innermost worlds.

Their laughter, now softened by the dawn, intertwined with the melodies of birdsong outside, harmonizing with the promise of a new day. With a lingering kiss, they embraced the inevitable transition from night to day, holding onto the memory of their shared journey through the depths of passion.

The candle, once the sentinel of their fervour, now stood as a sentinel of memories. Its wax had transformed with time, just as they had transformed in each other's presence. What had ignited as a flame of curiosity and attraction had now grown into a glowing ember of something deeper, something profound.

As they rose from their haven, they carried with them the residue of their intimate odyssey. Their footsteps marked the threshold of a new chapter, one that held the potential for more shared laughter, more whispered confidences, and more stolen moments.Delacey's waist.

Amid the soft glow of the candlelight, Trevor and Delacey found themselves caught in the rhythm of the music, their movements graceful and effortless. The strains of a melodic tune filled the air, carrying them away into a world where the worries of the day seemed to dissipate.

As they danced, their eyes locked, a silent understanding passing between them. It was in moments like these that Trevor felt a deep connection with Delacey, a bond that went beyond words. Her presence was a balm to his often chaotic life, a haven of tranquillity he could always count on. The flickering candles cast playful shadows on the walls, enhancing the intimacy of the setting. Trevor's fingers traced gentle patterns on Delacey's back, his touch sending shivers down her spine. Their laughter mingled with the music, filling the room with an infectious joy.

With a subtle change in tempo, the music shifted to a more mellow melody. Trevor pulled Delacey closer, their bodies now moving in a slow, sensual sway. Time seemed to slow down as they lost themselves in each other's arms, their hearts beating in sync.

As the song drew to a close, Trevor and Delacey held each other close, their breaths intermingling. In the hush of the moment, Trevor leaned in, his lips brushing against Delacey's forehead. The tenderness of the gesture spoke volumes, conveying a depth of emotion that transcended the boundaries of ordinary romance.

With a soft smile, Delacey looked up at Trevor, her eyes reflecting the warmth and affection she felt. In that shared gaze, they found solace and strength, a reminder that no matter the challenges that lay ahead, they could face them together.

The night pressed on, filled with exchanged tales and gentle mirth, as the flickering candlelight enveloped their moments in a tender, amorous radiance. As the hours passed, they retreated to the bedroom, where their passion ignited, and they savoured an exquisite journey of intimate connection.

In that intimate space, time lost its meaning, and the world outside faded into insignificance. Every touch, every whispered word, ignited sparks that set their senses ablaze. Fingers traced pathways of anticipation along skin flushed with emotion.

Chapter Ten

As time flowed onward, several weeks drifted away, and Trevor fully immersed himself in the mission of aiding Fall Two Inc. in reconstructing its once-magnificent realm. The orchestrated encounter between Trevor, Ariana, and their team emerged as a pivotal juncture. Plans were meticulously devised, creative concepts were born through brainstorming, and a shared resolve to resurrect the corporation's former grandeur enveloped the atmosphere. This culminated in a definitive choice to amalgamate the enterprise with InFall, giving rise to the new entity known as InFall Inc. The workforce from both realms united harmoniously, sparking a journey of not only domestic but also international ascendancy for the company.

Amidst this amalgamation, a sense of unity pervaded the halls of InFall Inc. Employees from both sides seamlessly merged their talents, forging a symbiotic relationship that transcended geographical boundaries. Collaborative efforts bore fruit as fresh ideas merged with established expertise, propelling the company's resurgence on a global scale.

As InFall Inc. burgeoned, its success story echoed far beyond its home turf. International markets welcomed the company's innovative products and forward-thinking strategies with open arms. Trevor's dedication and foresight, combined with Ariana's strategic acumen, became the driving forces behind this renaissance.

However, the path to greatness was not without its challenges. Rivals sought to undermine InFall Inc.'s rapid rise, and internal hurdles tested the mettle of the merged workforce. Yet, a shared sense of purpose and unwavering determination fortified their resolve to overcome these obstacles.

Within the intricate tapestry of corporate politics and global commerce, Trevor and Ariana found themselves not only as business leaders but also as architects of a profound transformation. The story of InFall Inc.'s ascent became a narrative of reinvention, resilience, and the potent results of visionary collaboration.

As the pages of the novel turned, the legacy of Trevor, Ariana, and the entire InFall Inc. family continued to evolve. Their journey served as a testament to the notion that even the mightiest empires could crumble, only to be reborn with newfound strength through the fusion of minds, the courage to embrace change, and the audacity to dream beyond convention.

Trevor's world was shaken when an unexpected letter arrived, beckoning him to a prestigious award ceremony. The contents revealed his nomination as a trailblazing maven in the realm of fashion and technology. Oblivious to the fact that victory was already his, he embarked on a journey from Seattle to Paris, accompanied by Delacey, to partake in the grand event that would forever alter his fate. As the plane touched down in the City of Light, Trevor's heart raced with a blend of excitement and trepidation. The bustling streets of Paris seemed to hum with anticipation, echoing his own inner turmoil. Delacey, ever the steadfast companion, stood by his side, a reassuring presence amidst the whirlwind of emotions.

As they navigated their way through the cobbled alleys and

charming boulevards, Trevor's thoughts danced between memories of his humble beginnings and the meteoric rise that had led him to this moment. He couldn't help but reflect on the countless nights spent tirelessly crafting his designs, merging technology with fashion in ways the world had never seen before.

The venue for the ceremony stood like a beacon of promise, its grandeur a stark reminder of the recognition that awaited him. Trevor's nerves grew more palpable with each step closer to the event, yet Delacey's words of encouragement served as a soothing balm to his anxious soul.

As they entered the venue, the air was thick with anticipation. Elegant gowns and impeccably tailored suits adorned the attendees, each a testament to the allure of the fashion world that Trevor had helped reshape. The atmosphere was electric, charged with a blend of camaraderie and competitiveness, as nominees vied for their moment in the spotlight.

The moment arrived. Trevor's name resonated through the hall, accompanied by a symphony of applause. He walked to the stage with a mixture of grace and humility, the weight of his achievements settling upon him like a crown. The award was presented, the culmination of years of dedication and innovation. The audience's admiration was tangible, a collective recognition of his groundbreaking contributions.

In his acceptance speech, Trevor acknowledged the power of collaboration, the fusion of creativity and technology that had brought him to this pinnacle. He spoke of the passion that had driven him to traverse continents, and he dedicated the award to the dreamers and risk-takers who dared to reimagine the boundaries of possibility.

As the ceremony concluded and the attendees mingled, Trevor found himself surrounded by peers and admirers, each seeking a moment to share their appreciation and perhaps glean a fragment of his insight. Delacey stood by his side, a silent pillar of support, her pride in him evident in the glint of her eyes.

The night unfolded like a dream, a symphony of laughter, achievement, and celebration. Amidst the festivities, Trevor realized that this was not just a recognition of his accomplishments, it was a validation of the path he had chosen, a testament to the beauty that could be born at the intersection of fashion and technology.

Beneath the canvas of the Parisian night sky adorned with countless stars, and amidst the radiant tapestry of city lights that danced on, Trevor and Delacey strolled along the captivating avenues. These were the streets where their shared moments overflowed with joy and lightheartedness. Yet, as fate often guides its own course, their footsteps led them to an inevitable juncture: beneath the luminous splendour of the Eiffel Tower. In this very spot, where Trevor had meticulously orchestrated his proposal, their destinies converged.

As they stood beneath the iconic arches of the Eiffel Tower, its intricate lattice of ironwork seemingly framing their emotions, a palpable sense of anticipation hung in the air. The gentle breeze whispered secrets of the night, carrying with it the echoes of laughter and shared confidences that had woven their connection.

For Trevor, this was a culmination of not just their journey through the labyrinthine streets of Paris, but also of the intricate path they had traversed in each other's hearts. His heart thrummed with a mix of excitement and nervousness, the weight of the ring in his pocket a constant reminder of the profound question he was about to pose.

Delacey, her eyes reflecting the flickering lights around them, sensed a shift in the atmosphere. She felt the weight of the moment, as if the universe itself had paused to witness their story. Every corner they had turned, every smile they had shared, seemed to have led them inexorably to this pivotal instant.

As Trevor took a deep breath, his gaze met Delacey's, and a lifetime of emotions passed between them. The symphony of their past echoed in their eyes, and the promise of their future shone like a beacon in the darkness. He knelt down on one knee, holding out the ring with a vulnerability that spoke volumes of his love.

"Delacey," his voice trembled, "From the first time we wandered these enchanting streets to this very moment beneath the stars, my heart has found its home in you. Will you continue this journey with me as my partner, my confidante, and my love?"

Time seemed to stand still as Delacey held her breath, her heart beating in sync with the pulse of the city around them. Tears glistened in her eyes as she nodded, a radiant smile breaking across her face like the dawn of a new day. "Yes, a thousand times yes!"

Applause seemed to erupt from the very soul of Paris itself, as if the city celebrated their union. The Eiffel Tower, witness to countless tales of love, stood tall, its lights shimmering with an extra hint of magic on this unforgettable night. Trevor slipped the ring onto Delacey's finger, sealing their commitment in a timeless embrace.

And so, beneath the celestial canvas of stars and amidst the romantic embrace of Paris, Trevor and Delacey embarked on a new chapter of their story, a chapter woven with love, destiny, and the promise of an everlasting bond. With each passing day, their bond deepened, like roots finding their way through rich soil. Their love story unfolded like a symphony, with crescendos of laughter, tender moments that lingered like a gentle breeze, and harmonious conversations that danced like melodies in the air. Paris became more than a backdrop, it became a character in their narrative. The Eiffel Tower witnessed their stolen kisses and heartfelt promises, while the Louvre seemed to acknowledge their love's timeless beauty. Amongst the city's sprawling parks and enchanting gardens, they discovered havens of serenity where they could relish moments intertwined. In due course, their path led them on a voyage homeward, drawing them back into the welcoming arms of Seattle. Trevor engaged in a heartfelt conversation with Delacey, the two weaving intricate plans for their upcoming nuptials. Envisioning their matrimonial celebration on the sun-kissed shores of Santorini, Greece, they dreamt of an intimate affair, surrounded by their dearest friends and beloved family. Their hearts danced with anticipation as they delved into the myriad details that would shape their destination wedding. Trevor and Delacey envisioned a ceremony that would transcend the ordinary, a union celebrated amidst the stunning backdrop of Santorini's azure skies and crystalline waters. With each passing day, their excitement grew, fueled by the prospect of uniting their lives in a place of such breathtaking beauty. The thought of sharing their vows against the backdrop of Santorini's iconic sunset filled them with a sense of enchantment that words could scarcely capture.

As they meticulously planned each aspect of their special day, from the delicate decorations to the carefully curated menu, their connection deepened. Hours were spent pouring over photographs of venues, researching local traditions, and envisioning the joy that would radiate from their cherished friends and family gathered to witness their love.

In the midst of the preparations, they discovered that the journey of planning their wedding was as much a celebration of their relationship as the day itself would be. The laughter they shared, the compromises they made, and the dreams they intertwined were all threads weaving a tapestry that would forever hold the story of their love.

Their lives now filled with anticipation, they eagerly awaited the moment when they would stand hand in hand on the shores of Santorini, ready to exchange vows that would bind them not only to each other, but also to the memory of this enchanting journey that had brought them to this point.

Chapter Eleven

As the calendar pages turned and the days flowed like a gentle current, the countdown to their Santorini wedding drew closer. The final touches were meticulously applied, ensuring that every aspect of their celebration resonated with the essence of their love story.

Trevor and Delacey's shared vision extended beyond the ceremony itself. They arranged excursions for their guests, inviting them to explore the island's hidden gems, bask in its rich history, and savour its delectable cuisine. With every itinerary item chosen, they hoped to create a collective experience that would etch this celebration into the hearts of their loved ones.

The rhythm of life seemed to harmonise with their anticipation. Even Seattle, with its familiar embrace, seemed to whisper its blessings as it prepared to bid them adieu once more. And so, as the day of departure neared, their suitcases were packed not only with clothes and essentials, but also with dreams, aspirations, and a shared determination to embrace this new chapter of their lives.

The journey itself became a voyage of introspection and connection. As they travelled to distant shores, they found themselves reflecting on the journey that had brought them to this point. Each place they visited, each encounter with locals and fellow travellers, served as a reminder of the vast tapestry of humanity they were now woven into.

The shores of Santorini greeted them with their radiant beauty. The island seemed to shimmer with an otherworldly glow, as if it recognized the significance of this moment. The anticipation of their wedding day was now a tangible presence, filling the air with excitement and magic.

As the sun dipped below the horizon, casting hues of gold and pink across the sky, Trevor and Delacey stood hand in hand, gazing at the sea. In that tranquil moment, they felt the culmination of their journey, the merging of their individual paths into one shared destiny. And as they looked ahead to the dawn of their wedding day, their hearts beat in unison with the rhythm of the waves, a harmonious prelude to the celebration that awaited them.

With the first light of the wedding day painting the sky in soft pastels, Trevor and Delacey woke to a sense of wonder that surpassed even their most vivid dreams. The island seemed to whisper its blessings as a gentle breeze carried the scent of blooming flowers and the distant melodies of morning birds.

Amidst the serenity of dawn, they prepared to step into a day that held the promise of forever. The air was imbued with a sense of reverence as they exchanged handwritten letters, pouring their hearts onto paper, each word a testament to the depth of their affection.

As the hours ticked by, the island gradually transformed. The chosen venue, nestled atop a cliff overlooking the Aegean Sea, was adorned with delicate drapery and vibrant florals that mirrored the hues of the ocean below. Guests arrived, their eyes reflecting both the beauty of the scenery and the joy of witnessing this love story unfold.

The ceremony itself was a symphony of emotions. With their closest friends and beloved family surrounding them, Trevor and Delacey professed their vows under the boundless expanse of sky. As their voices intertwined, promising love, support, and endless companionship, the sun seemed to stand still, casting a golden halo around them.

And then came the moment they had dreamt of, the exchange of rings, the timeless symbol of their commitment. With each touch of metal against skin, they sealed a promise that transcended time and place. The guests, seated in awe, felt the gravity of the moment as if the universe itself bore witness.

As the sun began its descent, painting the sky in a canvas of warm hues, the celebration shifted to a realm of joyous revelry. Laughter, music, and the clinking of glasses filled the air, a chorus of celebration that echoed their happiness. The feast that followed was a fusion of flavours, a testament to their journey that had led them here, to this vibrant crossroads of cultures and emotions.

Under the starlit Santorini sky, Trevor and Delacey took to the dance floor for their first dance as a married couple. Their steps were confident, each move a reflection of their shared rhythm, a dance of souls entwined. And as they swayed to the music, they knew that this day was not an ending, but a beginning, a portal into a future filled with shared dreams, challenges, and the unwavering support of each other.

The night grew older, the celebration continuing well into the early hours, fueled by love and the enchantment of the island. As their friends and family gathered around, the couple released paper lanterns into the night sky, each carrying a wish for their journey ahead.

And as the lanterns soared, their flickering lights blended with the stars, creating an illustration of hope and unity.

Trevor and Delacey watched, their hearts full, knowing that their love story was now forever etched into the tapestry of Santorini, a part of its history and its magic, a tale of two souls who dared to dream and found their happily ever after in a place where dreams truly came to life.

In the days that followed the grand celebration, Trevor and Delacey found themselves exploring the island's hidden corners, hand in hand. Santorini's narrow pathways led them through charming villages, past blue-domed churches, and down to secluded beaches where they revealed themselves in the solitude of the sea.

Their love seemed to deepen with every shared moment, every whispered secret, and every stolen glance. The island itself became a cherished witness to their post-wedding bliss, a silent confidant to their promises and dreams.

Chapter Twelve

As their time on Santorini drew to a close, they carried back more than just memories. The island had imprinted itself on their souls, a reminder that love could be as timeless as the waves that lapped at its shores.

The following dawn greeted them with a serene poolside breakfast. As the morning sun painted the scene in golden hues, they leisurely readied their belongings, bidding farewell to Santorini aboard the Sliteo and Delacey cruiser. Under the embrace of the sun's warm caress, they cruised amidst the glistening waves, revelling in the sun-kissed weather. They were filled with a renewed sense of purpose, determined to carry the magic of their destination wedding into the fabric of their everyday lives.

Amid this picturesque backdrop, a tender moment blossomed as Trevor's lips met Delacey's in a gentle kiss. Their companionship deepened as they relished each other's company. Yet, in the midst of this intimacy, Delacey's gaze fell upon the faint scars adorning Trevor's body. Concern etched her features, and she inquired about their origin.

Trevor, usually reticent, hesitated for a moment, then began to recount the painful tale. His voice trembled as he revealed that the burns on his skin were a painful reminder of his past. He shared how, during his childhood, his father's recklessness had led to a scalding incident involving boiling water. The scars that now adorned him were the physical vestiges of that traumatic event.

As his words hung in the air, a wave of emotions swept over Trevor, leaving him vulnerable. Delacey, sensing his pain, extended her gentle solace. She drew him close, her touch a comforting embrace. With unwavering empathy, she pressed a tender kiss upon his scars, a gesture of acceptance, compassion, and an unspoken promise of healing.

In the wake of that intimate exchange, their connection blossomed into a deeper understanding that transcended mere words. Each passing moment aboard the cruiser seemed to carry an air of renewal and transformation, as if the vast expanse of the sea itself held the power to mend wounds and renew spirits.

As the sun journeyed across the sky, casting its warm glow upon the sea's surface, Trevor found himself opening up in ways he had never before. With Delacey's patient and caring presence by his side, he recounted more tales from his past, each confession a step towards unburdening himself from the weight of his scars, both seen and unseen. Delacey, in turn, shared fragments of her own life's tapestry, creating a mosaic of shared experiences, vulnerabilities, and aspirations. They laughed about the small triumphs, exchanged advice on navigating life's challenges, and found solace in the quiet moments of reflection that the open sea provided.

As the cruiser sailed on, their story became a dance of healing, vulnerability, and hope. It was as if the waves themselves whispered promises of rejuvenation and second chances. In the gentle caress of the wind and the rhythm of the waves, Trevor and Delacey discovered the strength to heal not only from their past wounds but also from the doubts and insecurities that had held them back. As the sun began its descent, casting an array of colours across the horizon, Trevor and Delacey stood hand in hand, facing the expanse of the sea with a newfound sense of resilience. The scars that had once seemed like insurmountable barriers were now symbols of their shared journey towards acceptance and growth. And as the sun dipped below the edge of the sea, it marked not an end but a beginning, a beginning of a chapter in their lives where they could move forward together, embracing the healing power of love, understanding, and the boundless expanse of the sea that had borne witness to their transformation.

As they disembarked from the cruiser, Trevor and Delacey carried with them not just memories of breathtaking landscapes and tranquil moments but also the unbreakable bond they had formed. Their journey had shown them the power of vulnerability, the magic of healing, and the strength that arises when two hearts entwine with unwavering support.

They returned to the embrace of their home, hearts brimming with the richness of shared moments and the currency of affection. The tapestry of their joyous interlude lingered as they slipped back into their familiar rhythms. Weariness clung to them both, yet Trevor, ever the tender soul, bestowed upon Delacey a soothing massage that unravelled the knots of fatigue. As her eyelids surrendered to heaviness and dreams, his lips brushed her forehead in a silent benediction, a prelude to his gentle orchestration of warmth by tucking her under the blanket's embrace.

Meanwhile, Trevor found solace in the jacuzzi's bubbling waters, a haven of contemplation. The ripples mirrored the currents of his thoughts, for amid the marvels of his recent sojourn, an ominous missive from Ava had loomed, a declaration that the company's fate hung in the balance, precariously tethered to the weight of an unpaid loan. Lost in this tumult, his furrowed brow cast shadows over his features.

It was then that Delacey, sensing his disquiet like a note out of tune, emerged from the folds of privacy, shedding the trappings of modesty to join him in the waters. Her lithe form pressed against his, a human question mark, arms encircling him as if to shield him from the unseen assailant of worry. Her voice, soft as a whispered promise, breached the silence with the simple query, "Trevor, what weighs upon you?"

His response, a silent embrace followed by the delicate meeting of lips upon her forehead, spoke of a wordless communion. Words, it seemed, were inadequate vessels for his turmoil. And so, in the embrace of the jacuzzi's embrace, they embarked on a journey of unspoken solace, a shared space where the nuances of affection painted the canvas of concern in hues of quiet strength and shared happiness.

As the waters of the jacuzzi cradled them, the symphony of their unspoken connection played on. Trevor's fingers traced delicate patterns on Delacey's back, an unvoiced conversation etched in touch. Each stroke conveyed a reassurance, a vow that their partnership was unyielding against the storm that threatened to unfurl.

Delacey nestled closer, her breath mingling with his in the steamy air, a tender counterpoint to the turbulence of their circumstances. In this intimate tableau, time seemed to ebb and flow at a pace known only to lovers and dreams. She tilted her head, catching his gaze, her eyes beckoning him to open up the wellspring of his thoughts.

His lips parted, as if to spill the words trapped within

his chest, but then he paused, a wistful smile tugging at the corners of his mouth. Instead, he began to speak of the sunrises that had greeted him on his recent journey, painting the sky with hues that defied the constraints of language. He recounted encounters with strangers who had become friends and the landscapes that had whispered secrets to his soul. And with each word, his voice wove a tapestry of escape, a momentary respite from the weight of impending decisions.

Delacey listened, her heart attuned not just to his words but to the cadence of his emotions. She sensed his desire to protect her, to keep the burdens of the world at bay, and yet she also understood that they were partners, facing life's challenges together. When the narrative of his adventures wound to a gentle close, she leaned in, her lips brushing against his, an affirmation that their shared journey was as vital as any solitary exploration.

As the evening stars emerged overhead, they remained entwined in the jacuzzi's embrace, their bodies relaxed, their spirits intertwined. The weight of uncertainty still lingered, but in that fleeting moment, it felt less formidable. Love, after all, was their compass, guiding them through uncharted waters. They emerged from the bubbling jacuzzi, drying their feet before heading to bed. Nestled closely, they embraced and entwined, drifting into slumber in each other's arms. Under the soft glow of the moonlight seeping through the curtains, their breathing synchronized as they journeyed through dreams. Each held a world of their own, yet intertwined in the realm of sleep, their minds danced on ethereal threads that only lovers could fathom. As the night deepened, a gentle breeze rustled the curtains, its cool caress a stark contrast to the warmth shared between them. The room seemed to hold its breath, as if preserving the sanctity of their connection. Time lost its grip as their dreams intermingled, creating a tapestry of shared experiences and unspoken emotions. In this intimate cocoon, worries and troubles of the waking world faded into insignificance. The complexities of life dissolved, leaving behind only the pure essence of their bond. A stray thought might have brushed against them, a fleeting reminder of responsibilities and obligations, but it was swiftly carried away on the currents of serenity that enveloped their slumber. The night wore on, stars twinkling in the velvet sky, mirroring the constellations they formed in each other's arms. Their entwined figures seemed like a sculpture crafted by the universe itself, a testament to the timeless art of love. As dawn approached, the first soft light of morning brushed against their faces, and their dreams slowly released their grip. Their embrace loosened, yet their connection remained steadfast. With a sigh that held both reluctance and contentment, they began to stir, awakening from the world they had woven together in the tapestry of the night.

With fluttering eyelids and sleepy smiles, they gazed at each other, still caught between two realms. Reality beckoned, but the magic of the night lingered, an intangible reminder that their love was a force beyond the ordinary.

And so, they emerged from the cocoon of sleep, their entwined spirits carrying the essence of the night into the daylight hours. Ready to face the world anew, they stood united, their love a constant flame that would guide them through the impending journey.

Chapter Thirteen

Back within the loving embrace of their cherished city, Trevor and Delacey discovered themselves encircled by the familiar, though every aspect carried an air of novelty. Their affection had deepened, their connection had solidified. They embraced their roles as companions, now harbouring a newfound gratitude for the path they had undertaken.

Life followed its cadence, punctuated by trials and victories, yet the memory of their wedding in Santorini remained a beacon, a wellspring of motivation that underscored the limitless potential of their love. Their dwelling transformed into a haven, a realm in which they nurtured their aspirations, a blank canvas onto which they painted their shared destiny.

As their eyes lingered upon the photograph from their Santorini wedding, prominently showcased in their living space, their lips curved into smiles, stirred by the recollections it encapsulated, the mirth, the tears, the vows, and the pledge of an eternity together.

Trevor departs for his office, only to find a scene of utter chaos upon his arrival. With a sense of urgency, he reaches out to every member of the InFall Inc workforce, summoning them for an impromptu meeting. The aim is clear: devise a strategy to overcome the overwhelming debt that has ensnared him. The origins of this predicament elude him, yet Trevor joins forces with his adept financial team to confront the challenge head-on, their collective minds forging a path toward a solution.

As the employees of InFall Inc gather in the conference room, tension hangs heavy in the air. Trevor paces at the front, his usually composed demeanour now tinged with a sense of urgency. The flickering fluorescent lights cast an eerie glow on the faces of his team, reflecting the uncertainty of the situation.

"Thank you all for coming," Trevor begins, his voice steady despite the turmoil inside him. "I know the chaos outside might mirror the chaos within us, but we're here to find a way out of this predicament."

A murmur of agreement ripples through the room. Personnel engage in apprehensive gazes, some fidgeting with pens or shuffling papers in their hands. Trevor's reputation as a visionary leader has never been tested like this before.

"As you're aware," Trevor continues, "we're facing a debt that seemingly appeared out of nowhere. But dwelling on the 'why' or 'how' won't get us far. We need solutions—innovative, decisive strategies that will not only clear our path but also reaffirm our standing."

His words resonate with the team. Trevor's unwavering resolve starts to kindle a spark of hope amidst the uncertainty.

Turning to his financial team, Trevor nods, giving them the floor. The Chief Financial Officer steps forward, projecting graphs and figures onto the screen. With calculated precision, he outlines the scale of the debt and potential consequences if left unchecked.

"But it's not just about mitigating loss," he emphasises. "We have an opportunity to reposition ourselves, to find new avenues of growth and redefine our identity."

As ideas start flowing, the atmosphere in the room transforms. Creativity begins to overshadow the fear of failure, and a collective determination takes root. One by one, employees share suggestions, ranging from restructuring internal processes to exploring untapped markets.

Trevor is deeply engrossed, intermittently nodding in acknowledgment and inquiring for further elaboration. He's not just a CEO in these moments, he's a conductor harmonizing a symphony of diverse voices, each contributing a unique note to the composition of recovery. Hours pass, but the energy remains undiminished. The emergency meeting evolves into a collaborative brainstorming session, a testament to the resilience of the InFall Inc team. Trevor's steadfast leadership empowers his employees, reminding them that adversity can be a crucible for innovation.

As the meeting draws to a close, a sense of accomplishment washes over the room. The initial chaos has given way to a collective determination—a shared belief that they can overcome any challenge thrown their way. Trevor looks around at his team, a mixture of exhaustion and hope in their eyes.

"We might not have all the answers yet," he says, his voice carrying a newfound strength, "but together, we have the power to forge a new path. Let's continue working on these ideas and reconvene soon."

The team disperses, each member infused with a renewed sense of purpose. Trevor observes their departure, feeling a surge of gratitude for their dedication. As he remains in the conference room, the flickering lights no longer seem ominous, they're a reminder that even in the darkest moments, there's always a way to illuminate the path forward.

In the days that follow, Trevor and his team work tirelessly, turning the ideas generated during the emergency meeting into actionable plans. The office becomes a hub of focused activity, with departments collaborating in ways they never have before. Walls are covered with charts, post-it notes, and diagrams, representing the intricate web of strategies being woven together.

Trevor finds himself deep in conversation with his financial team. They pore over financial statements, projections, and potential risk scenarios. Together, they refine the approach, ensuring that every decision is backed by data and a clear understanding of the market dynamics. Simultaneously, the marketing and product development teams spring into action. They devise innovative campaigns to rejuvenate interest in their offerings, exploring uncharted territories and targeting demographics previously overlooked. Trevor is impressed by the fervour with which his employees have embraced this challenge, transforming a seemingly insurmountable obstacle into an opportunity for reinvention.

In the midst of this focused effort, Trevor also discovers a sense of camaraderie among the employees. The emergency meeting served as a catalyst for deeper connections, breaking down hierarchical barriers and fostering an environment where everyone's voice is valued. The coffee machine conversations and impromptu brainstorming sessions in the hallway become integral to the collaborative spirit that's driving the company forward.

As weeks turn into months, the collective efforts begin to yield results. InFall Inc starts to see signs of a turnaround, increased customer engagement, positive media coverage, and a notable uptick in sales. Trevor is cautious but hopeful, he understands that this is just the beginning of a long journey, but the progress is undeniably encouraging.

During a follow-up meeting with his team, Trevor takes a moment to reflect on how far they've come. He stands before them once again, the conference room now a symbol of triumph rather than chaos. The atmosphere is charged with a sense of accomplishment as they review the milestones achieved and set new targets.

"We've demonstrated that even in the face of adversity, we can adapt, evolve, and emerge stronger," Trevor states, his voice resonating with pride. "This journey has reaffirmed that our greatest asset is not just our products or services,it's the incredible people who make up the heart of InFall Inc."

They've not only weathered a storm but also transformed it into a voyage of discovery, innovation, and growth. The debt that once seemed insurmountable now serves as a reminder of their resilience and ability to navigate uncharted waters. And at the heart of it all is Trevor, a leader who not only guided his team through a crisis but also fostered a sense of unity and purpose that would forever shape the company's trajectory.

It was truly remarkable witnessing Trevor and his enterprise flourishing. Yet, on a specific day, while seated at his desk, an idea germinated in his mind—to extend an invitation to Delacey, urging her to assume the role of company president. In due course, he summoned Ava to his office, instructing her to contact Delacey and present her with this enticing job proposition.

With mounting anticipation, Ava punched in the number. After a few rings, the warm voice of Delacey greeted her with a pleasant "hello." Following a brief exchange of pleasantries, Ava took the lead, her words carrying a gentle eagerness, "How have things been at your end, Delacey?" Delacey replied, her tone infused with familiarity, "I must say I've been quite well, Ava. Now, what's the occasion for this call?" Brimming with excitement, Ava conveyed, "I bring forth excellent news. Following meticulous contemplation and extensive discussions with Mr. Trevor, we are absolutely thrilled to let you know that he is wholeheartedly on board with the proposition. Your exceptional talents have not only been acknowledged, but we've also received commendations from a former board member of your previous company."

Chapter Fourteen

Delacey's heart skipped a beat at Ava's words. The news seemed to hang in the air, a delicate promise of something entirely unexpected. She cleared her throat, her voice a mix of astonishment and curiosity, as she prodded further, "Accepted the idea? Talents? Former board member? Ava, you're leaving me in suspense here."

Ava couldn't help but chuckle at Delacey's eagerness. "Apologies for the suspense, Delacey. What I mean to say is that Mr. Trevor and the entire company recognize your incredible abilities. Your reputation precedes you, even catching the attention of someone from your past corporate realm who had nothing but praise for you. The offer on the table is nothing short of a prestigious role as the president of the company."

Delacey's mind whirled with a whirlwind of emotions. A mixture of surprise, disbelief, and a hint of elation surged through her veins. She had spent years climbing the corporate ladder, honing her skills, and here was a chance to leap onto a new precipice altogether.

As the seconds ticked by, Delacey's voice trembled with a blend of gratitude and astonishment. "Ava, I don't know what to say. This is... unexpected. And incredibly humbling. Please convey my gratitude to Mr. Trevor for even considering me."

Ava's smile was evident in her tone as she replied,

"I'll definitely do that, Delacey. But know that this offer comes not just from Mr. Trevor, but from everyone who recognizes the value you bring. We believe you're the missing piece to take the company to greater heights."

Overwhelmed by the weight of the moment, Delacey leaned back against her chair, her eyes unfocused as she envisioned the possibilities. "Thank you, Ava. I'll need a little time to think this through, but please let Mr. Trevor know how deeply honoured I am."

"Of course, Delacey. Take your time. We're eager to have you on board, but the decision is entirely yours. When you're ready, we can arrange a meeting to discuss the details."

As they exchanged a few more pleasantries, Delacey's mind raced, weaving the threads of her past and present into a tapestry of an uncertain yet exciting future. She hung up the phone, her thoughts spinning, heart racing, and a new chapter awaiting her, one she had never anticipated but was now ready to embrace. Delacey reached out to Ava via phone, expressing her readiness to commit to the company's endeavours.

As plans fell into place, a meeting was scheduled, where intricate details would be unveiled and the ink would meet paper on Delacey's contract with the company. Trevor, her spouse, couldn't help but wear an expression of profound contentment. The sight of his wife ascending to the position of company president brought immense joy to Trevor, marking a transformative chapter in their lives. The prospect of sharing not merely a coexistence in life but also an odyssey in the professional realm filled him with pride.

Their journey had led them to this pivotal juncture, a moment that shimmered with the promise of change and growth. Delacey's call to Ava, with its resolute commitment, set the wheels in motion for a new phase in their lives.

A sense of anticipation hung in the air as they counted down the days to the meeting. Trevor, ever the supportive partner, admired Delacey's determination. He saw in her a leader, someone who could bring fresh perspectives and innovative ideas to the company's realm.

However, just a day before the scheduled meeting, an unexpected email arrived. It was from a rival company, offering Delacey a position of even higher authority and a chance to lead a groundbreaking project. The timing was impeccable, and the temptation was undeniable.

As Delacey grappled with this unexpected twist, she found herself torn between loyalty to the company she had initially chosen and the allure of a new challenge that promised greater recognition and influence. Trevor, sensing her inner conflict, stood by her side, offering his unwavering support without pushing her in either direction.

The day of the meeting arrived, tension palpable in the air. Delacey walked into the conference room, her mind a whirlwind of thoughts. The decision she was about to make could reshape not only her professional trajectory but also the dynamics of their relationship.

As the discussions unfolded and the moment to sign the contract approached, Delacey's gaze shifted between the document before her and the email that still lingered on her mind. With a deep breath, she picked up the pen and made her choice.

The applause that followed was a mix of relief and excitement. Trevor's smile, though tinged with a hint of curiosity, was genuine. Walking out of the meeting, hand in hand, Delacey and Trevor knew that the road ahead wouldn't be without its challenges. Yet, this twist had injected a new sense of purpose into their journey. As they navigated the complexities of their intertwined personal and professional lives, they were more determined than ever to make their story one of resilience, ambition, and love.

In the aftermath of her decision, Delacey's mind was a maelstrom of emotions. The path she had chosen diverged from the one she had initially envisioned, opening up a realm of possibilities she hadn't anticipated. Trevor's unwavering support was a balm to her uncertainty, his presence a constant reminder that they were in this together.

As news of Delacey's choice spread through the company, reactions were mixed. Some admired her courage in staying true to her commitment, while others whispered about the rival offer she had turned down. It was a stark reminder of the scrutiny that often accompanied such pivotal decisions.

In the days that followed, Delacey plunged into her new role with fervor. Challenges emerged, and she tackled them head-on, drawing upon her ingenuity and determination. Trevor, ever the optimist, became her sounding board and confidant, offering insights and encouragement as she navigated uncharted waters.

As the months passed, Delacey's leadership began to bear fruit. Her innovative strategies revitalised the company, leading to unprecedented growth and success. The initial scepticism that had surrounded her decision gradually transformed into admiration and respect. Trevor watched with a mix of pride and awe as his wife forged a path that was uniquely hers.

Yet, with success came new complexities. The demands

of Delacey's position consumed her time, sometimes overshadowing the moments she and Trevor used to cherish. Late nights at the office and business trips became the norm, leaving them little time for their personal lives.

One evening, as they sat across from each other at their dining table, the weight of their busy lives hung in the air. Trevor gently broke the silence, his voice laced with concern. He spoke of their journey, the twists that had brought them here, and the need to find equilibrium in the midst of their ambitions.

Delacey's expression softened as she realized the toll her dedication was taking on their relationship. In that moment, they made a pact to rediscover the balance that had drawn them together in the first place. They started setting aside time for each other, nurturing their bond amidst the whirlwind of responsibilities.

Their story continued, now marked not only by their individual successes but by their joint pursuit of a life that seamlessly intertwined their personal and professional aspirations. The twist that had once threatened to pull them apart had, in fact, become the catalyst for their mutual growth, reminding them that no matter the challenges, they were stronger together.

Delacey and Trevor found themselves facing a formidable challenge that neither could have foreseen. A series of industry shifts and economic turbulence rocked the business landscape, putting their company's stability in jeopardy. The very foundation they had worked so hard to strengthen seemed to tremble.

Delacey's strategic acumen was put to the ultimate test. Long nights and intense brainstorming sessions became the norm once again, but this time, they were punctuated by shared glances and unspoken reassurances between her and Trevor. The adversities they encountered became a crucible, forging an even deeper connection between them. Trevor's unyielding support never faltered, and he became a beacon of unwavering optimism during even the darkest moments. Their conversations were a blend of business strategy and personal reflections, an acknowledgement that their lives were intricately woven together, both in the boardroom and at home.

As the storm raged on, they devised a daring plan that defied conventional wisdom. It was a risky move that could either salvage the company or amplify the damage. With a mix of trepidation and audacity, they presented their plan to the board and rallied their team to execute it flawlessly.

The days that followed were tense, filled with anticipation and anxiety. Every development, every small victory or setback, was shared between Delacey and Trevor. Their bond was their anchor amidst the turmoil, a reminder that they were a team not just in their relationship but also in their shared pursuit of success and resilience.

Slowly but steadily, their plan began to bear fruit. The company weathered the storm, emerging stronger and more resilient than ever before. The triumph was a testament not only to Delacey's strategic brilliance but also to Trevor's unwavering belief in her and their shared vision.

As they stood together, surveying the renewed vigour of their company, there was a profound sense of accomplishment that enveloped them. The twists and turns of their journey had taught them that while challenges could be daunting, they were opportunities in disguise, opportunities to grow individually and as a couple.

Their story continued to unfold, marked by the highs and

lows of business and life. Through it all, Delacey and Trevor remained a united front, navigating the unpredictable waters with resilience, love, and an unshakable partnership.

Chapter Fifteen

The moment of savouring had arrived—the long-awaited vacation. After relentless days and nights of unwavering dedication, they had successfully attained their desires.

They could finally bask in the fruits of their labour, luxuriating in this well-deserved respite. The toil and sweat they had poured into their pursuits had paid off, granting them the satisfaction of reaping what they had sown. This was their opportunity to unwind, their moment to relish the rewards that their hard work had earned.

In the tranquil embrace of the vacation, they found solace from the bustling demands of their daily grind. The persistent grindstone they had pressed against had now been set aside, replaced by a serene landscape of relaxation. In the midst of the tranquil morning, Trevor's heart skipped a beat as he glanced at Delacey's phone. He couldn't shake off the unease that her ex-boyfriend's messages brought, a reminder of a chapter they both wished to forget. Determined not to let it cast a shadow over their time together, Trevor sighed and put the phone back down. The tennis court awaited, a sanctuary where Trevor could channel his thoughts and emotions into each swing of the racket. As he rallied with the ball, the rhythmic thumping of his heart seemed to synchronize with his movements. The crisp sound of the ball meeting the strings resonated like a melody, helping him momentarily tune out the world's distractions.

On the sidelines, Delacey watched with a mixture of admiration and concern. She knew that the past still had a hold on both of them, its grip stubborn and unyielding. She longed to bridge the gap that the memories of ex-relationships had left behind. Yet, she understood that healing was a process that took time, patience, and mutual support.

After the tennis session, their energies spent, they retreated to a quiet spot overlooking the golf field. The lush expanse stretched before them, a canvas of green tranquillity. Trevor, his breath returning to a steady rhythm, finally spoke, his voice carrying the weight of his thoughts.

"Delacey, I can't help but feel unsettled when I see those messages from your ex-boyfriend. It's as if he's a spectre from the past, trying to disrupt our present."

Delacey gazed at him, her eyes softening with understanding. "Trevor, I wish I could erase that part of my past entirely. But those scars have shaped who I am today. What matters is that I'm here with you now, working to build something new."

Trevor nodded, appreciating her honesty. "You're right. We can't change what's already happened, but we can choose how we let it affect us. Let's focus on the moments we're creating together and leave the shadows where they belong."

As the sun climbed higher in the sky, its warmth enveloping them, Trevor and Delacey shared a smile, a silent agreement passing between them. They knew that healing required effort, but they were committed to supporting each other in facing the remnants of their pasts. Hand in hand, they walked away from the shadows of yesterday, stepping into the embrace of a promising future, ready to create new memories that would eventually outshine the scars of yesterday.

It was evening, as the sun began its descent, casting a warm orange glow across the horizon, Trevor and Delacey found themselves on a leisurely stroll around the serene golf field. The cool breeze whispered through the trees, carrying with it a sense of renewal.

"You know, Trevor," Delacey began, her voice gentle, "I used to think that my past was a burden I had to carry alone. But being with you has shown me that we can lighten each other's loads by sharing our stories."

Trevor nodded, his gaze fixed on the setting sun. "It's not easy to open up about our vulnerabilities, especially when they're tied to painful memories. But there's strength in our willingness to confront them together."

They walked in silence for a while, the air growing cooler as the sky transitioned into a canvas of deep purples and blues. The past was a mosaic of experiences, some fractured and painful, others beautiful and cherished. Trevor realized that acknowledging the shadows of their past didn't diminish the light they were building in their present.

As they reached a bench overlooking the golf course, Delacey turned to Trevor, her eyes earnest. "I want you to know that you're not alone in this journey. Whatever ghosts from the past haunt us, we have the power to exorcize them together."

Trevor's heart swelled with gratitude for her understanding. He reached for her hand, their fingers intertwining, a symbol of their unity in facing the remnants of their history.

"Delacey, every day I spend with you reaffirms my belief in the beauty of new beginnings," Trevor confessed, his voice steady and sincere. "The scars may always be there, but they remind us of our strength to heal and love again."

With the moon rising overhead and the stars beginning to twinkle, Trevor and Delacey sat together, gazing out at the expanse before them. The scars of yesterday were transforming into stories of triumph, and as they leaned into each other's embrace, they embraced the promise of a future that held the potential to outshine even the brightest sunsets. Delacey commented, "You see, if something is destined for you, it will find its way back to you. And if it doesn't, then it was never meant to be a part of your life." Trevor felt a sense of bewilderment, interpreting it as an indication of a weakening connection. Trevor's heart weighed heavily with Delacey's words. As he looked out the window, lost in thought, he couldn't help but replay her statement in his mind. Was it really a sign of their bond faltering? Or was it just a philosophical musing? He had always believed in the strength of their connection, the way they understood each other without needing many words. But now, doubt crept in like a shadow, casting uncertainty over everything they had built together. Trevor had seen relationships around him crumble, heard stories of love slipping through fingers like sand. Could that be their fate too?

He turned the words over and over, trying to extract their true meaning. Did Delacey mean that their bond was slipping away? Or was she merely speaking about life in general, the ebb and flow of destinies? Trevor yearned for clarity, for a way to know whether he should fight for what they had or let it go.

The days that followed were a tumultuous whirlwind of

emotions. Trevor found himself watching Delacey closely, searching for any signs that she was pulling away. He clung to her words, dissecting them for hidden messages, and he scrutinized their interactions for any hint of distance. Their once effortless conversations now felt laden with unspoken tension.

Yet, amidst the confusion, Trevor also recognized the danger of overthinking. Maybe Delacey's words were simply a reminder to cherish what they had, to appreciate the present moment instead of worrying about an uncertain future. He knew that relationships required effort, nurturing, and the willingness to weather storms together.

One evening, as they sat under a canopy of stars, Trevor finally gathered the courage to address the elephant in the room. "Delacey," he began, his voice soft but steady, "I've been thinking about what you said the other day."

Delacey turned to him, her eyes reflecting the glimmer of the moon. "I knew it was on your mind," she replied gently.

Trevor took a deep breath. "I realize now that I've been so focused on the idea of losing us that I forgot to focus on what we have. Our bond is important to me, and I want to do whatever it takes to nurture it."

A tender smile curved on Delacey's lips. "Trevor, I'm glad you brought this up. My words were more about the beauty of embracing the present than about predicting our future. If anything, they were a reminder that what truly matters is how we treat each other now."

Trevor nodded, a sense of relief washing over him. At that moment, he understood that he didn't need to decode every word or look for hidden meanings. Their bond wasn't something to be held by fear, but to be cherished through mutual understanding and care.

As they gazed at the stars above, hand in hand, Trevor felt a renewed sense of connection with Delacey. The universe might be full of uncertainties, but what they shared was their own story to shape. And as long as they continued to nurture their bond, it would remain a constant, guiding them through whatever lay ahead.

$$\mathit{To\ be\ continued...}$$

However, as life's unpredictable nature dictates, circumstances can take a harsh and unexpected turn. Following their delightful journey, they find themselves back at their abode, only to be greeted by a more intricate and sorrowful reality. Delacey pays another visit to her former partner, while Trevor tirelessly scours every corner in search of her, yet her elusive presence remains unattainable. The narrative unfolds as Delacey embarks on an expedition alongside Mateo, her previous beau.

Trevor's relentless pursuit of Delacey mirrors the desperation of a man consumed by longing. Every unturned stone and uncharted avenue deepens his determination to reunite with her, painting a vivid picture of his devotion against the canvas of uncertainty. As Delacey and Mateo's journey unfolds, they find themselves traversing both physical landscapes and the landscapes of their own hearts. The echoes of their past resonate with every step, casting shadows on their present choices and prompting them to contemplate the roads they have taken. Amidst the twists and turns of this novel's rich tapestry, themes of love, loss, and the resilience of the human spirit come to the forefront. With each chapter, the characters' stories interweave, creating a mosaic of emotions and experiences that resonate with the reader's own journey through life's unpredictability.

79

Acknowledgement

I extend my heartfelt gratitude to the many individuals who have supported me throughout this incredible journey of writing and publishing my book. Without their unwavering encouragement, guidance, and belief in my abilities, this endeavour would not have been possible.

First and foremost, I would like to express my deepest appreciation to my family. Your endless love, patience, and understanding have been the pillars of my strength. Thank you for always encouraging me to pursue my passions and for instilling in me the value of hard work and determination.

To my friends and mentors, thank you for your invaluable support and guidance. Your insightful feedback and encouragement have been instrumental in shaping my writing and pushing me to new creative heights. I am forever grateful for your presence in my life.

I am indebted to the team at Fall Two Inc, Croiretre, and The Webasing, whose collective effort and dedication have made this book a reality. Your expertise and commitment to excellence have been truly inspiring.

Thank you for believing in my vision and for working tirelessly to bring it to fruition.

I would like to express my gratitude to the editors

and proofreaders who have contributed their time and expertise to refine the manuscript. Your meticulous attention to detail and insightful suggestions have elevated the quality of this book.

A special thank you goes to the readers and supporters of my poetry. Your words of encouragement and the connection we share through the written word have been a constant source of inspiration. It is my hope that this book resonates with you, just as your support has resonated with me.

Finally, I want to thank all those who have played a part, big or small, in shaping my journey as a writer and entrepreneur. Your belief in my abilities has fueled my passion and motivated me to strive for excellence.

To each and every individual who has touched my life and contributed to this book, please accept my sincerest gratitude. Your presence in my journey is cherished and your support is deeply valued.

Infallible Two

Infallible Two is a riveting story about unplanned interactions and the strength of love that overcomes all obstacles. Trevor Cartier, still buzzing after the energetic party, meets Delacey Dunne, an elusive woman. After being brought together by fate, they set off on an epic voyage of sharing moments, insecurities, and undeniable attraction. As their bond grows stronger, they realize that their chance encounter was not a coincidence but rather the beginning of a love story foretold by the stars. In a world where fate appears inevitable, Trevor and Delacey's relationship is a testament that true love transcends all limits.

Unerring Two: Longing And Heartscapes

Trevor's relentless pursuit of Delacey mirrors the desperation of a man consumed by longing. Every unturned stone and uncharted avenue deepens his determination to reunite with her, painting a vivid picture of his devotion against the canvas of uncertainty. As Delacey and Mateo's journey unfolds, they find themselves traversing both physical landscapes and the landscapes of their own hearts. The echoes of their past resonate with every step, casting shadows on their present choices and prompting them to contemplate the roads they have taken. Amidst the twists and turns of this novel's rich tapestry, themes of love, loss, and the resilience of the human spirit come to the forefront.

Elegisticaire: An Elegist's Journey Through Eloquent Emotions

A captivating collection of poetic musings that takes you on a profound journey through the realms of emotion, imagination, and lyrical expression. In this enchanting anthology, the talented wordsmith behind Bardicaire invites you to immerse yourself in a tapestry of beautifully woven verses that dance gracefully upon the pages.

With meticulous craftsmanship, each poem encapsulates the essence of human experiences, evoking a wide spectrum of emotions, from the bittersweet whispers of love and longing to the triumphant crescendos of hope and resilience. Through the artistry of language, the poet paints vivid landscapes of the heart, exploring themes of nature, introspection, and the mysteries of the soul.